SHERLOCK HOLMES

THE STOCKBROKER'S CLERK

SIR ARTHUR CONAN DOYLE

Sweet Cherry

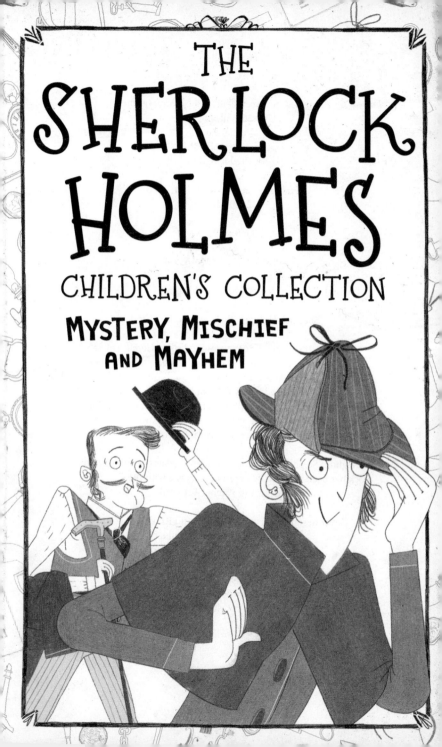

Published by Sweet Cherry Publishing Limited
Unit 36, Vulcan House,
Vulcan Road,
Leicester, LE5 3EF
United Kingdom

First published in the UK in 2020
2020 edition

2 4 6 8 10 9 7 5 3 1

ISBN: 978-1-78226-659-4

Cover design by Arianna Bellucci and Rhiannon Izard
Illustrations by Arianna Bellucci

www.sweetcherrypublishing.com

Printed and bound in China
C.WM004

Most people would not believe that a person's slippers held secrets. But on a wet June morning my dear friend, Sherlock Holmes, proved to me that they did.

I was sitting in my surgery, reading *The British Medical Journal* after breakfast.

Quite out of the blue, I heard a ring at the doorbell. It was followed by the shrill voice of Sherlock Holmes.

'Ah, my dear Watson,' he said, striding into the room. 'I am delighted to see you! I hope that Mrs Watson is well?'

'Thank you, we are both very well,' I said, standing up and shaking Holmes warmly by the hand.

'I also hope that you have not entirely lost interest in our little investigations? Even though you are busy running your own surgery?' he asked. He took off his hat and put it on the table, then sat down in the rocking chair.

I sat down again too.

'Quite the opposite,' I said. 'Just last night I was looking over my old notes. I thought I should put our past cases into some sort of order.'

He frowned. 'I hope you don't consider the collection closed?'

'Not at all. I would like nothing better than to have another of our adventures.'

'Today, for example?'

Holmes gave me a small smile.

I nodded. 'Yes, today, if you like.' I felt a thrill of excitement.

'And as far off as Birmingham?'

'Certainly, if you wish.'

'And what about your patients?'

'My neighbour is also a doctor. I see his patients when he's away. He is always ready to do the same for me.'

'Ha! Nothing could be better,' said Holmes, leaning back in his chair. He looked keenly at me from under his half-closed eyelids. 'I see that you have been unwell lately. Summer colds are always a little annoying.'

'I had to stay in for three days last week with a bad chill. I thought that I'd lost all trace of it.'

'So you have. You look remarkably fit,' Holmes replied.

'Then how could you tell?'

His smile widened into a smug grin. 'My dear fellow, you know my methods.'

'You deduced it, then?' I asked.

'Certainly.'

'And from what?'

'From your slippers.'

I glanced down at the new shiny brown leather slippers that I was wearing. 'How on earth ...' I began. But Holmes answered my question before it was asked.

'Your slippers are new,' he said. 'You could not have had them more than a few weeks. But the soles I see are slightly scorched. For a moment, I thought that they might have got wet and been burned in the drying. But near the heel there is still a small piece of paper with the name of the shop on it. If the slippers got wet, this would have fallen off. So logic then states that you must have been sitting with your feet stretched out to the fire. A man would not do this if he were well, even in such a wet June as this. You *must* have been ill.'

I laughed. Like all of Holmes' reasoning, it seemed simple once it was explained. He read the thought on my face, and his smile had a tinge of annoyance.

'I'm afraid that I rather give myself away when I explain my reasoning,' he said. 'Results without reasons are much more exciting and mysterious. Are you ready to come to Birmingham, then?'

I stood up eagerly. 'Certainly. What is the case?'

'We shall tell you about it on the train. My client is outside in a cab. Can you come at once?'

'In an instant.' I scribbled a note for my neighbour and rushed upstairs to tell my wife where I was going. Then I grabbed my coat and hat from the stand and joined Holmes on the doorstep.

'So, this is the neighbour who is a doctor,' he said, looking at the brass plate next to the one with my name on.

'Yes. He bought his practice the same time as I did. Both have been here since the houses were built.'

'Ah, then you got the better of the two practices,' said Holmes.

'I think I did, but how do you know?'

'By the steps, my friend. Yours are worn three inches deeper than his.'

I smiled at his deduction. He was quite right. Far more people had used my steps than my neighbour's.

As we opened the door of the carriage, Holmes said, 'I would like to introduce you to my client, Mr Hall Pycroft.'

I shook hands with the man as I climbed in and sat down.

Holmes followed me and then leaned forwards. 'Hurry along, cabby. We have only just enough time to catch our train.'

The man sitting opposite me was a well-built young fellow.

He had an honest face and a small, yellow moustache. He wore a very shiny top hat and a neat black suit. His outfit made him look like what he was – a smart young city man. His round face seemed naturally cheerful, but the corners of his mouth were pulled down as though something were worrying him.

It was not until we were on the train to Birmingham that I learned why Mr Pycroft's face seemed so unnaturally worried.

'We have a journey of just over an hour,' said Holmes. 'I want you, Mr Hall Pycroft, to tell my friend about your very interesting experience. Repeat it exactly as you told it to me, or with even more detail if possible. It will be useful for me to hear the order of events again.'

Holmes turned to me. 'Watson, this is a case that may prove to have something in it, or it may prove to have nothing. It does seem to be the kind of puzzle that you and I both like.'

He turned back to the man.

'Now, Mr Pycroft, please go ahead.'

Mr Pycroft looked at me with a twinkle in his eye.

'The worst part of the story is that I show myself to be such a fool,' he said. 'Of course, it may work out all right. And, really, I don't see that I could have done anything else. But if I've lost my job over this, I shall feel that I've been a real idiot.

'I must also say that I'm not very good at telling stories, Doctor Watson, but I'll try.

'I used to have a job at Coxon and Woodhouse's financial company, in Draper's Gardens. They suffered in the financial crash and had to let go of all the clerks, all twenty-seven of us. I tried desperately to get another job, but there were so many people doing the same thing that it was very difficult.

'I had been earning three pounds a week at Coxon's, and I had saved about seventy pounds. But that money was soon gone. In the end, I could hardly scrape together enough to buy stamps to answer the job advertisements. I had worn out my boots climbing up office stairs and yet seemed no nearer to getting another job.'

I nodded, feeling glad that doctors were always needed.

Pycroft continued. 'At last I saw a vacancy at Mawson & Williams, the great stockbroking company in Lombard Street. You may not know much about it, but it is one of the richest businesses in London. The advertisement was to be answered by letter only. I sent in my reference and

Stockbroking

A man can get very rich from stockbroking. Stocks are small parts of businesses. If a person buys stock, then they own a part of that business. A stockbroker helps people buy and sell these stocks, just as a shopkeeper helps people buy milk or bread.

application, but did not think I had a hope of getting the job.

'They answered my letter, saying that if I would go there next Monday I could begin the new job at once. I have no idea why they chose me from all the applicants they must have had, but I was very pleased. The salary was one pound a week more than my old job and the work did not seem any more difficult.'

I smiled, wondering where his story was going. Holmes sat in the corner of the seat with his head resting against the window and his eyes closed. He looked half asleep, but I knew he was listening intently.

'And now comes the strange part of the business,' went on Pycroft, sitting forwards in his seat. 'It was the very evening after I had received my job offer. I was sitting in my room, in Hampstead, when my landlady came in. She said that I had a visitor, and gave me his card.

Arthur Pinner
Financial Agent

I had never heard of the name Arthur Pinner before and could not imagine what he wanted. But, of course, I asked her to show him up.

'He was a medium-sized man with dark hair, dark eyes, a shiny nose and a black beard. He moved very quickly and spoke sharply.

'"Mr Hall Pycroft, I believe?" he said.

'"Yes, sir," I answered, pushing a chair towards him.

'He took it and then looked at me.

'"You used to work at Coxon and Woodhouse? Is that right?"

'"Yes, sir," I replied.

"'And you are now on the staff of Mawson & Williams?'"

"'Yes.'"

"'Well,' he said, 'the fact is that I've heard some stories about you. Stories about how clever you are with money. Do you remember Parker, the manager at Coxon and Woodhouse? He says a lot of good things about you.'"

A light shade of pink grew across Pycroft's cheeks. He was clearly not used to compliments.

'Of course, Doctor Watson, I was very pleased to hear this. I had always been pretty sharp in the office, but I had never dreamed that I was talked about in this way.'

He went on with his story.

'"Do you have a good memory?" Pinner asked me.

'"Pretty fair," I answered.

'"Have you kept up to date with the financial market while you've been out of work?"

'I nodded eagerly. "Yes, of

course! I read the stock exchange list every morning."

"'That is the way to prosper!" he cried. "You won't mind me testing you, will you? Let me see. How is the Ayrshire stock?"

"'A hundred and six and a quarter to a hundred and five and seven eighths."

Stock exchange
Small parts of businesses, known as stocks, are sold on the stock exchange. It is like an invisible shop, where all the stocks are kept and bought and sold from. Newspapers will regularly print a long list of all the stocks and how much they are worth.

"'And New Zealand Consolidated?'"

"'A hundred and four.'"

"'And British Broken Hills?'"

"'Seven to seven and six.'"

"'Wonderful!'"

he cried, with

his hands up.

"My boy, you are

much too good

to be a clerk at

Mawson &

Williams!"

'This really

surprised me, as you can imagine. "Well, other people don't think as much of me as you seem to do, Mr Pinner," I said. "I had a hard enough fight to get this job, and I'm very glad to have it."

"'Pooh, man, you could do much better! Now, what I can offer you is still not enough for a man of your talents, but it's far better than measly Mawson's. Let me see. When do you start at Mawson & Williams?"

"'On Monday.'"

"'Ha ha! I will bet that you don't go there at all.'"

"'Not go to Mawson & Williams?'"

"'No, sir. By then you will be the business manager of the Franco-Midland Hardware Company. We have one hundred and thirty-four branches in the towns and villages of France. That's not counting one in Brussels and one in San Remo.'"

'This took my breath away. "I have never heard of it," I said.

'"No. The business has been kept very quiet – it's too good a thing to let the public into. My brother, Harry Pinner, is the managing director. He knew I was down here and asked me to pick up a good man. A young, ambitious man with sharp wits. When Parker told me how talented you were, I knew I had to meet you myself. We can only

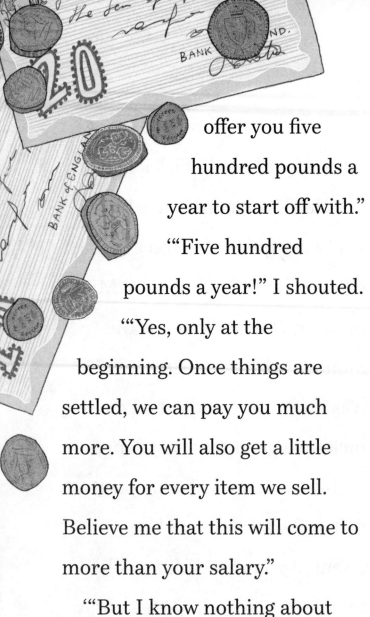

offer you five hundred pounds a year to start off with."

"'Five hundred pounds a year!" I shouted.

"'Yes, only at the beginning. Once things are settled, we can pay you much more. You will also get a little money for every item we sell. Believe me that this will come to more than your salary."

"'But I know nothing about

hardware. I could hardly tell you the difference between a cake plate and a teacup."

'"No, my boy, you know about numbers."

'My head buzzed with excitement. I could hardly sit still in my chair. But suddenly a little chill of doubt came over me. The job seemed too good to be true.

'"I must be honest with you," I said. "Mawson & Williams only pays me two hundred, but

Mawson & Williams is safe. I don't know anything about your company …"

"'Ah, smart, smart!" he cried delightedly. "You are the very man for us. You are not easily persuaded, and quite right, too. Would one hundred pounds change your mind? If you *would* like to join us, you can just put it into your pocket, as an advance on your salary."

"'That's very generous," I said. "When will I start my new job?"

"'Be in Birmingham tomorrow at one o'clock," he said. "I have a note here for you to take to my brother. You will find him at 126B Corporation Street, at the temporary offices of the company. Of course, he must agree to you being hired, but I know it will be all right."

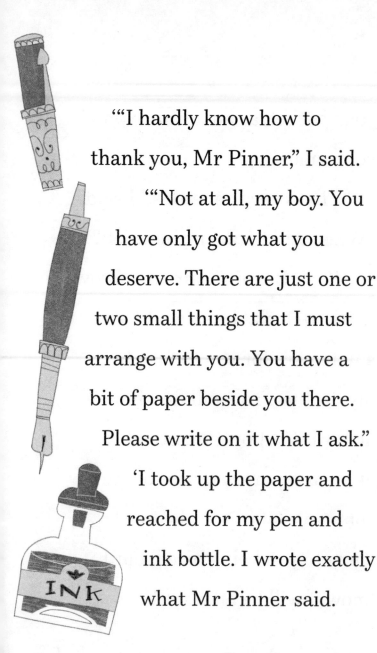

'"I hardly know how to thank you, Mr Pinner," I said.

'"Not at all, my boy. You have only got what you deserve. There are just one or two small things that I must arrange with you. You have a bit of paper beside you there. Please write on it what I ask."

'I took up the paper and reached for my pen and ink bottle. I wrote exactly what Mr Pinner said.

40

I am perfectly willing to act as business manager for the Franco-Midland Hardware Company, at a minimum salary of £500.

Mr Hall Pycroft

'After I finished writing, Mr Pinner took the paper and put it into his pocket.

'"There is one other detail," he said. "What are you going to do about Mawson & Williams?"

'I had forgotten all about Mawson's in my joy. "I'll write and resign," I told him.

'"Exactly what I don't want you to do. I had a row over you with Mawson & Williams' manager. I went to ask him about you, and he was very rude.

He accused me of stealing you away from his company. Finally, I lost my temper. 'If you want good men you should pay them a good wage,' I said.

""He would rather have our small wage than your big one,' he answered.

""I'll bet you a fiver that when he has seen my offer, you'll never hear from him again,' I said.

""Done!' he said. 'We picked him out of the gutter. He won't leave us so easily.' Those were his very words."

'"The cheeky rogue," I cried. "I've never even met him. Why should I think about him in any way? I will certainly not write if you don't want me to."

'"Good," he said, getting up from his chair. "Well, I am delighted to have got such a good man for my brother. Here's your advance of one hundred pounds. And here is the letter to give to my brother."

'I took out my notebook and made a note of the address.

126B Corporation Street, Birmingham. 1pm.

"'Good night," said Pinner, "and may you have the fortune you deserve."

'Then Mr Pinner shook my hand and left. You can imagine,

Doctor Watson, how pleased
I was. What an amazing bit of
good luck! I sat up half the night
celebrating. Then, the next day I
was off to Birmingham on a train
that would get me there in plenty
of time for my appointment. I
took my things to a hotel in New
Street. Then I went to the address
that had been given to me.'

I looked at Pycroft. He took a
deep breath before continuing
his story. I knew that it would

probably end badly. He would not be here otherwise. But he was in no way a stupid man.

'I was fifteen minutes early for my appointment, but I did not think it would matter. 126B was a passage between two large shops. It led to a winding stone stairway. A long list of names was painted on the wall. But I could not see the name Franco-Midland Hardware Company among them. I stood there for a few minutes feeling very disappointed. I was wondering whether the whole thing was a big con, when a man came up and spoke to me. He was very much like the man I'd seen the night before. He had the same figure and the same voice, but he had no beard and his hair was lighter.

'"Are you Mr Hall Pycroft?" he asked.

'"Yes," I said.

"'Oh, I was expecting you, but you are a bit early. I had a note from my brother this morning. He says you're a very talented man."

"'I was just looking for the offices when you came."

"'We haven't got our name up yet, because we only rented this office last week.

Come up with me and we'll talk
the matter over."

'I followed him to the top of
the stairway. There, right under
the roof, were a couple of empty,
dusty little rooms, with no
carpets and no curtains.

'He led me in. I had imagined
a great office with shining tables
and rows of clerks, as I was used
to. I must have stared rather sadly
at the two chairs and one little
table. Apart from a ledger and

a small bin, they were the only things in the room.

'"Don't be disappointed, Mr Pycroft," said the man, seeing the look on my face. "Everything starts small. We have lots of money behind us, though our offices are not much to look at yet. Please sit down and let me have your letter."

'I gave it to him, and he read it over carefully.

Dear Harry,

May I recommend to you the bearer of this letter, Mr Hall Pycroft. He comes with excellent references and would seem perfect for the job.

Arthur

"'You seem to have made a big impression on Arthur, my brother," Mr Harry Pinner said. "And I know that he's a pretty wise judge. This time I shall follow his advice. You definitely have the job."

"'What are my duties?" I asked.

"'You will eventually manage the great depot in Paris. It will pour a flood of English crockery into the shops of France. Everything from plates and bowls to teacups and butter dishes," Harry Pinner explained. "The deal will be completed in

54

a week. But, for now, you will stay in Birmingham and make yourself useful."

'"How?"

'To answer my question, he took a big red book out of a drawer.

'"This is a directory of Paris. It lists the names of every person in the city, along with their job," the

brother said. "I want you to take it home with you and to mark off all the crockery sellers, with their addresses. It would be very useful to have them."

"'Surely there are already lists of companies?" I said.

"'Not reliable ones," Harry Pinner said. "Their system is different from ours. Let me have the lists by Monday, at twelve o'clock. Good day, Mr Pycroft. If you continue to show eagerness and intelligence, you will do well in this company."

'I went back to my hotel with the big book under my arm and with very mixed feelings. On the one hand, I definitely had the job and one hundred pounds in my pocket.

On the other hand, the look of the offices, the strange task and the absence of their name on the wall made me think things were not quite right.

'Whatever happened, I had my money, so I settled down to my task. I worked every minute of Sunday, yet by Monday

I had only got as far as H. I went again to the dusty offices. I told my employer how much progress I had made, and was told to just keep working on the task until Wednesday. Then I should come back again.

'On Wednesday it *still* wasn't finished. So I worked until Friday – that is, yesterday. Then I brought it round to Mr Harry Pinner.

'"Thank you very much," he said. "The task was much more

difficult than I thought. The list
will be a great help to me."

"'It took a long time," I said.

"'And now I want you to make
a list of the furniture shops too.
They all sell crockery
as well."

"'All right," I replied.

"'Come back
tomorrow evening
at seven o'clock
and let
me know

60

how you are getting on. Don't overwork yourself. A couple of hours at the music hall this evening would do you good."

'He laughed as he spoke. I was shocked to see that his second tooth on the left-hand side had been filled with gold.'

Sherlock Holmes rubbed his hands with delight. Once again I was baffled. I had no idea why this was important. I stared at our client.

'You may well look surprised, Doctor Watson,' he said. 'But when I was speaking to Mr Arthur Pinner, in London, I noticed that his tooth was filled in the exact same way. The glint of the gold caught my eye both times, you see. I put the pieces together in my head. The same voice, the same figure, the same tooth – the only things that were different were the beard and hair. And that could have been

done by a razor and a wig. I was
absolutely sure that the two
brothers were the same man!

'Of course, you expect two brothers to look alike. But you do not expect them to have the same tooth, filled in the same way. My mind was a whirl as the so-called Mr Harry Pinner showed me out. I found myself in the street hardly knowing whether I was on my head or my heels. I went back to my hotel and splashed my face with cold water, to clear my head.

'Why had he sent me from London to Birmingham? Why

had he got there before me?
Why had he written a letter from
himself to himself? It was all too
much for me. I could make no
sense of it.

65

'And then it struck me. I
thought that what was a puzzle
to me might be clear to Mr
Sherlock Holmes. So, here I am.'

We paused for a moment. Then
Holmes glanced at me and leaned
back on the cushions. His face
looked pleased and yet critical –
as if he had just tasted a very rich
cake and was trying to decide
whether he liked it or not.

'Rather fine, Watson, isn't
it?' he said. 'There are points in

it that please me. I think that an interview with Mr Arthur-Harry Pinner would be rather interesting for both of us.'

'But how can we do it?' I asked.

'Oh, easily enough,' said Hall Pycroft, cheerily. 'You are two friends of mine who need a job. What could be more natural than me bringing you both to meet the managing director?'

'Exactly,' said Holmes. 'I would like to have a look at the

gentleman and see if I can make anything of his little game. What qualities do you have, my friend, that would make your services so valuable? Or is it possible that …'

Holmes drifted off and began

biting his nails and staring blankly out of the window. We hardly got another word from him until we were in New Street Station.

68

We had a late lunch. Then we spent the afternoon strolling about the city and resting at Pycroft's hotel.

At seven o'clock that evening the three of us walked to the company's offices.

'It is no use being at all early,' said our client. 'He must only come there to see me, because the place is empty until the time he says.'

'That is an important point,' said Holmes.

'By Jove, I told you so!' cried Pycroft. 'That is him in front of us.'

He pointed to a smallish, dark, well-dressed man. He was rushing along the other side of the road. As we watched him, the man looked across at a newspaper boy. He was shouting out the headlines of the evening paper. The man ran desperately through a stream of cabs and buses to buy one. Then he vanished through a doorway,

clutching the newspaper in
his hand.

'There he goes!' cried Hall
Pycroft. 'Those are the company's
offices. Come with me!'

We followed Pycroft up five flights of stairs until we reached a half-open door. Pycroft tapped on the door.

A voice told us to enter. We walked into a bare, unfurnished room, just as Hall Pycroft had described. At the single table sat the man from the street. His evening paper was spread out in front of him. He looked up at us – I had never looked at a face that showed so much grief. And there was more than grief. There was horror.

His forehead shone with sweat. His cheeks were the dull, dead white of a fish's belly, and his eyes were wild and darting all over the place. He looked at his clerk as if he didn't recognise him. I could see by Pycroft's face that this was not how the man usually looked.

'You look ill, Mr Pinner!' exclaimed Pycroft.

'Yes, I am not very well,' Pinner answered. He tried to pull himself together, licking his dry lips as he spoke.

'Who are these gentlemen you have brought with you?' he asked.

'One is Mr Harris, of Bermondsey, and the other is Mr Price, from here in Birmingham,' said Pycroft. 'They are friends of mine and experienced gentlemen. They have been out of work for quite some time. They hoped that you might find a job for them in your company.'

'Very possibly! Very possibly!' cried Mr Pinner with a ghastly smile. 'Yes, I have no doubt that we shall be able to do something for you. What is your trade, Mr Harris?'

'I am an accountant,' said Holmes.

'Ah, yes, we shall need an accountant. And you, Mr Price?'

'A clerk,' I said.

'I'll let you know as soon as we have decided. But now I ask you to go. For God's sake, leave me alone!'

These last words were shot out of him, as if he'd been holding them back for some time.

Holmes and I glanced at each other. Hall Pycroft took a step towards the table.

'You forget, Mr Pinner, that I am here by appointment. I am supposed to receive some more orders from you,' Pycroft said.

'Certainly, Mr Pycroft, certainly.' Pinner's tone was calmer. 'Can you wait here a moment? Your friends can wait with you. I will be with you in three minutes. Please be patient for just a little longer.'

He stood up in a very polite way and bowed to us. Then he went through a door at the far end of the room and closed it behind him.

'What now?' whispered Holmes. 'Is he giving us the slip?'

'Impossible,' answered Pycroft.

'Why?' Holmes asked.

'That door leads into an inner room.'

Holmes stared at it. 'There is no exit?'

'None.'

'Is it furnished?' asked Holmes.

'It was empty yesterday.'

'Then what on Earth can
he be doing?' cried Holmes.
'There is something that I don't
understand in his manner.
He is almost mad with terror.
What can have made him so
frightened?'

'Perhaps he thinks that we are
the police,' I suggested.

'That's it,' cried Pycroft.

Holmes shook his head. 'But
he did not turn pale when he saw

us. He was pale when we entered the room,' he said. 'It is just possible that …'

His words were interrupted by a loud banging.

'Good gracious!' cried Pycroft. 'What is he doing in there?'

The banging came again. This time it was much louder. Then came a loud sobbing and a sudden scream that shot through my ears like a gun. We all locked our eyes on the closed door.

Glancing at Holmes, I saw his
face turn rigid.

Suddenly, Holmes sprang
across the room and pushed at the
door. It was locked on the inside.
Following him, we threw
ourselves on it with
all our weight.

One hinge snapped, then the other, and the door fell down with a crash. Rushing over it, we found ourselves in the inner room.

It was empty.

We paused for just a second before seeing the second door. Then Holmes sprang to it and pulled it open. A coat and waistcoat were lying on the floor. We looked over to the corner. There was the managing director of the Franco-Midland

Hardware Company. He was hammering his fists against the wall and screaming like a madman. Tears stained his pale cheeks and even more welled in his red eyes.

In an instant, I ran over and grabbed his wrists. His knuckles were cut and covered with blood from punching the wall. Holmes and Pycroft took one arm each and heaved him up. Then we carried him into the other room.

His face was the colour of clay. His lips shook as if he were going to start crying again. He was a dreadful wreck of the man that he'd been just five minutes before.

'What do you think, Watson?' asked Holmes.

I stooped over and examined him.

'He's not in a good way,' I said. 'Just open that window and hand me the water jug.'

I poured a little cold water over his face to try to calm him down. 'Lie down,' I told him, folding my jacket and placing it underneath his head. 'You need to rest.'

Holmes stood by the table, with his hands in his pockets and his chin on his chest.

'I suppose we should call the police,' he said. 'Yet I admit I would like to give them a complete story when they come.'

'It's a mystery to me,' said Pycroft, scratching his head. 'Whatever they wanted to bring me all the way up here for, and then ...'

'Pooh! All that's clear enough,' said Holmes. 'It's this last sudden

88

move that puzzles me.'

'You understand the rest, then?' said Pycroft, frowning.

'I think that it is fairly obvious,' said Holmes. 'What do you say, Watson?'

I shrugged. 'I must admit that I'm as much in the dark as Pycroft here.'

Pycroft gave me a small smile of thanks.

'Oh, surely if you think about the events, they can only point to one answer,' said Holmes. I tutted at his smugness. Holmes loved being smarter than everyone else – and reminding them of it!

'So how do you explain it?' Pycroft asked.

'Well, the whole thing hangs on just two points,' said Holmes. 'The first is making you write a statement, saying that you were

fectly willing to act
ess manager for the
idland Hardware
Limited, at a

90

joining this ridiculous company. Do you see what that means?'

Pycroft said nothing.

'I'm afraid I miss the point,' I answered.

Holmes turned to me.

'Well, why did they want him to write it down? These things are usually just spoken agreements at that point. Why should this time be different from the usual ways of doing things?'

He turned back to Pycroft. 'Do you see, my young friend? They wanted to get a sample of your handwriting. They had no other way of doing it.'

'Why did they want my handwriting?' Pycroft asked.

'Quite so. Why? When we answer that, we will be one step closer to solving this mystery. And there can be only one good reason. Someone wanted to learn to copy your writing.

'And now think about the second point. Pinner asked you not to resign your place at Mawson & Williams. He wanted the manager to think that a Mr Hall Pycroft – whom he had never seen – was coming to the office on Monday morning.'

'My God!' cried our client. 'What a blind beetle I have been!'

'Now you see the point about the handwriting. Your handwriting would have been

on your application form for
Mawson & Williams. So, if
someone was going to take your
job they had to have the same
handwriting. They could easily
pretend to be Mr Hall Pycroft,
as I bet no one in the office had
seen you yet.'

'Not a soul,' groaned Hall
Pycroft.

'Very good. Of course, it was
very important to stop you
changing your mind. Plus, they

had to keep you from meeting anyone who worked at Mawson & Williams. They could not risk you meeting anyone who could tell you that your double was working in the Mawson's office. So they gave you a generous advance on your salary, and sent you off to Birmingham. Then they gave you so much work that you had no time to go back to London. That is all plain enough.'

95

'But why should this man pretend to be his own brother?' I asked Holmes.

'Well, that is easily explained, also. There are clearly only two men in the crime. One is pretending to be you at the office. While this man, here, pretended to be both Mr Harry and Mr Arthur Pinner. To create a believable company, and get you up to Birmingham, he knew he would need two men at the head of the 'business'. But his partner was busy pretending to be you, and he did not want to bring anyone else in on the secret. So he tried to disguise himself by shaving and wearing a wig. If it were not for the gold tooth filling, you might have believed that they truly were brothers, rather than one person.'

Hall Pycroft shook his fists in the air.

'Good gracious!' he cried. 'So while I have been foolishly working up here, what has this other Hall Pycroft been doing at Mawson & Williams? What should we do, Mr Holmes? Tell me what to do.'

'We must send them a telegram,' Holmes replied.

'They close at twelve o'clock on Saturdays.'

'Never mind. There may be some doorkeeper or attendant ...'

'Yes, there is,' said Pycroft. 'There is always a guard on the door, to protect the valuable securities. Securities, of course,

---

Securities

These are the certificates that prove that a person owns stock in a business. They are worth a lot of money. If someone were to steal securities, they would really be stealing the stock, which they could then sell in secret.

are almost the same as cash. I remember hearing it talked of in the City.'

'Very good. We shall send a telegram to him. He can tell us if all is well, and if a clerk named Hall Pycroft is working there. That is clear enough. But what is not clear is why this rogue walked out of the room when he saw us and almost cried himself into a fit.'

'The paper!' croaked a voice behind us.

We all spun round.

The man was sitting up. His face was still pale and streaked with the drying tears. He had come back to his senses and rubbed nervously at his eyes.

'The paper! Of course!' yelled Holmes. 'I have been such an idiot! I didn't think about the paper. Of course, the secret must be there.'

He flattened it out on the table, peered over it and gave a cry of triumph.

'Look at this, Watson,' he cried. 'It is a London paper, an early edition of *The Evening Standard*. Here is what we want. Look at the headlines.'

THE EVENING

CRIME IN THE CITY.
MURDER AT MAWSON & WILLIAMS' OFFICE.
ATTEMPTED ROBBERY.
CAPTURE OF THE CRIMINAL.

'Here, Watson,' said Holmes, handing me the paper. 'We all want to hear it, so please read it aloud to us.'

I began to read the huge front-page story.

CRIME IN THE CITY.
MURDER AT MAWSON & WILLIAMS' OFFICE.
ATTEMPTED ROBBERY.
CAPTURE OF THE CRIMINAL.

A desperate attempt at robbery happened this afternoon in the City. It led to the death of one man and the capture of the criminal.

Mawson & Williams, the famous financial house, looks after securities that are worth well over a million pounds. The company keeps its precious securities in the very latest safes, and has an armed guard patrolling the building. But this was still not enough to keep criminals away.

Last week a new clerk named Hall Pycroft was taken on by the firm. This person is actually none other than Beddington, the famous thief. He and his brother had only just been released after a five-year prison sentence. By some means, which are not yet clear, Beddington used a false name to successfully gain a job in the Mawson & Williams' office. From there he was able to study the building and the locks on the safes. He knew exactly where the most valuable securities were kept.

As usual, the Mawson & Williams clerks left at midday on Saturday. Sergeant Tuson, of the City Police, happened to be passing the building that afternoon. He was quite surprised to see a gentleman with a large bag come down the steps at twenty minutes past one. Sergeant Tuson followed the suspicious-looking man. Then, with the help of Constable Pollack, succeeded in arresting him.

It was at once clear that a huge robbery had been committed. Nearly a hundred thousand pounds worth of American railway bonds were discovered in the bag.

On searching the Mawson & Williams building, the body of the armed guard was found, hidden in the largest safe. The guard had received a blow on the back of the head with a poker.

The police are sure that Beddington had been allowed back into the building after midday by pretending that he had left something behind. After he murdered the guard, he quickly emptied the safe and then made off with his stolen treasures.

Beddington's brother, who usually works with him, has not appeared in this crime, as far as is known. Police are tracking him down at present.

I looked up at Holmes and Pycroft.

'Well, we can save the police some trouble,' said Holmes, glancing at the haggard figure huddled up by the window. 'Human nature is a strange mixture, Watson. Even the evil Beddington has a brother here that loves him so dearly that he cannot stand the idea of him being caught. The news led him to completely break down.

'We have no choice as to what we must do. The doctor and I will remain on guard. Mr Pycroft, if you will please go out and call the police,' said Holmes.

Luckily for Mr Hall Pycroft, the managers at Mawson & Williams were very understanding. Once both the criminals were arrested and the story was explained, Pycroft was happily welcomed into his new job.

As to Holmes, he returned to 221B Baker Street, with a smug smile of achievement painted across his face.

'Another job well done, Watson,' he said, as he sat down to his coffee.